THE GARDEN PLOT

Don't miss any of the cases in the Hardy Boys Clue Book series!

#1: *The Video Game Bandit*

#2: *The Missing Playbook*

#3: *Water-Ski Wipeout*

#4: *Talent Show Tricks*

#5: *Scavenger Hunt Heist*

#6: *A Skateboard Cat-astrophe*

#7: *The Pirate Ghost*

#8: *The Time Warp Wonder*

#9: *Who Let the Frogs Out?*

#10: *The Great Pumpkin Smash*

#11: *Bug-Napped*

#12: *Sea Life Secrets*

#13: *Robot Rescue!*

#14: *The Bad Luck Skate*

Coming soon:

#16: *Undercover Bookworms*

HARDY BOYS

→Clue Book←

#15

THE GARDEN PLOT

BY FRANKLIN W. DIXON ⟺ ILLUSTRATED BY SANTY GUTIÉRREZ

ALADDIN

NEW YORK LONDON TORONTO SYDNEY NEW DELHI

ALADDIN

An imprint of Simon & Schuster Children's Publishing Division
1230 Avenue of the Americas, New York, New York 10020
First Aladdin paperback edition April 2022
Text copyright © 2022 by Simon & Schuster, Inc.
Illustrations copyright © 2022 by Santy Gutiérrez
Also available in an Aladdin hardcover edition.
All rights reserved, including the right of reproduction in whole or in part in any form.
ALADDIN and related logo are registered trademarks of Simon & Schuster, Inc.
THE HARDY BOYS, HARDY BOYS CLUE BOOK, and colophons
are registered trademarks of Simon & Schuster, Inc.
For information about special discounts for bulk purchases, please contact
Simon & Schuster Special Sales at 1-866-506-1949 or business@simonandschuster.com.
The Simon & Schuster Speakers Bureau can bring authors to your live event.
For more information or to book an event contact the Simon & Schuster Speakers Bureau
at 1-866-248-3049 or visit our website at www.simonspeakers.com.
Series designed by Karina Granda
Cover designed by Tiara Iandiorio
The illustrations for this book were rendered digitally.
The text of this book was set in Adobe Garamond Pro.
Manufactured in the United States of America 0322 OFF
2 4 6 8 10 9 7 5 3 1
Library of Congress Cataloging-in-Publication Data
Names: Dixon, Franklin W., author. | Gutiérrez, Santy, 1971- illustrator.
Title: The garden plot / by Franklin W Dixon ; illustrated by Santy Gutiérrez.
Description: New York : Aladdin, [2022] | Series: Hardy Boys clue book ; 15 | Audience:
Ages 6 to 9 | Summary: Detective brothers Frank and Joe investigate garden sabotage.
Identifiers: LCCN 2021021976 (print) | LCCN 2021021977 (ebook) |
ISBN 9781534476844 (hc) | ISBN 9781534476837 (pbk) | ISBN 9781534476851 (ebook)
Subjects: CYAC: Brothers—Fiction. | Mystery and detective stories. |
LCGFT: Detective and mystery fiction. | Novels.
Classification: LCC PZ7.D644 Gar 2022 (print) | LCC PZ7.D644 (ebook) |
DDC [Fic]—dc23
LC record available at https://lccn.loc.gov/2021021976
LC ebook record available at https://lccn.loc.gov/2021021977

CONTENTS

CHAPTER 1   READY, SET, GROW!   1

CHAPTER 2   FURRY FRENEMIES   8

CHAPTER 3   EDIBLE ENVY   18

CHAPTER 4   CUCUMBER CRIME SCENE   25

CHAPTER 5   FENCE DEFENSE!   32

CHAPTER 6   NEFARIOUS NEIGHBORLINESS   44

CHAPTER 7   MOUSE MANEUVERS   54

CHAPTER 8   WHY DID THE WOODCHUCK
             CROSS THE ROAD?   60

CHAPTER 9   PICK A PECK OF UN-PICKLED
             PEPPERS   65

CHAPTER 10   THE GOOD, THE BAD,
             AND THE BANANAS   81

THE GARDEN PLOT

Chapter 1

READY, SET, GROW!

"Gardening is the best," eight-year-old Joe Hardy said, leaning back in his lawn chair and munching on a freshly pulled carrot.

"There's a difference between eating the garden and gardening." His older brother, Frank, looked up from weeding the zucchini patch. "I'm the one doing most of the work. And if you keep eating all our veggies, there won't be anything left for the judges from the FEEL Contest to judge."

The Bayport Science Center was sponsoring the Friendly Environment Edible Lawn—FEEL for short—Contest. Just about all the houses in the Hardys' neighborhood had signed up to turn their front lawns into eco-friendly edible landscape gardens.

"It's an *edible* landscape contest. What good is a yard full of plants you can eat if you're not allowed to eat the edibles? Right, Mr. Bee?" Joe asked the bumblebee collecting pollen from one of the bright red nasturtium flowers growing along the path leading to the Hardys' front door. Joe plucked one of the petals and popped it into his mouth. "Who knew flowers could be so tasty?"

"The bees help by pollinating the plants," Frank said. "*You* just eat them!"

Joe shrugged. "By the way, the beans look like they could use some watering, when you get a chance." He took another bite of his carrot. "See, I'm helping!"

Joe pulled a leaf from a tall stalk with pom-pom-shaped purple flowers on top, but Frank started waving his hands in the air. "Don't eat the milkweed leaves! Not all parts of every plant are edible or okay to snack on raw. You should never try something unless you're totally sure."

Frank sighed. "Besides, the block party where they judge the contest is just a few days away, and I want to at least get an honorable mention. Even if we don't win, there are still a lot of great prizes for the runners-up."

"Our neighborhood sure has come a long way since they announced the contest a few months ago," Joe said, looking up and down their tree-lined street. "Before everyone started gardening this spring, the street was full of boring old grassy front lawns."

"All that water people were using just to grow grass no one can eat is now growing lots of food," Frank said. "Edible lawns look good *and* they're good for the planet."

"And tasty!" Joe said. "The whole street is like one big, beautiful garden full of munchies."

"Some of the yards are more beautiful than others."

Joe and Frank looked up to see their schoolmate Vic hop onto the curb in front of their house. He wore a fancy leather holster with a garden spade on one hip and a pruner on the other. His knees were covered in dirt, just like Frank's.

"Don't rub it in, Vic," Frank grumbled, looking across the street at the gorgeous edible jungle growing on Vic's front lawn.

"You gotta admit, it is pretty spectacular," Joe said. "The kale plants look like little palm trees! And check out all those cucumbers. There must be a hundred of them!"

He whistled at the six-foot-tall trellis next to Vic's house. It was made of carefully crisscrossed bamboo poles, and cucumbers of different colors, shapes, and sizes dangled from the green-leafed vines that were climbing up it.

Vic glanced across the street, admiring his garden. "Thanks, Joe. My family's always been known for our green thumbs. Your garden isn't bad either."

"It could be better," Frank said with a sad glance at the spotty patch of lettuce next to him.

"Everybody can't be the best at everything," Vic said, leaning on the Hardys' gated fence. "My family may be gifted gardeners, but everyone knows the Hardys are Bayport's best mystery solvers. Not that it's any mystery who's going to win the FEEL competition."

Vic looped his thumbs through the belt of his holster and grinned.

"Gardening is a new hobby for me, I guess," Frank said, looking down at the stack of gardening books and seed catalogs sitting next to his bin of tools.

The whole town knew about the Hardy boys' first hobby—detecting. Their dad, Fenton, was a detective, so like Vic's green thumb, it ran in the family.

"Us gumshoes make okay gardeners, but our specialty really is cracking cases," said Joe.

"What's a gumshoe?" Vic asked.

"It's an old-timey way of saying detective," Joe explained.

"The rubber on sneakers used to be called gum, so 'gumshoe' means an investigator who can sneak around and be stealthy," Frank added.

There was a sudden not-at-all-stealthy rustling from the bushes behind the garden. The three boys looked up to see the leaves shaking, like something was lurking inside them.

Vic bit his lip nervously. "Um, what is—"

Before he could finish his question, a wild beast burst into the yard!

Chapter 2

FURRY FRENEMIES

Vic yelped at the sight of the furry creature.

Frank gritted his teeth and growled.

Joe grinned and waved. "Hi, Woody!" he called to the pudgy brown animal as it waddled up to the fence behind the garden. It was the size of a very fat cat, with stumpy little legs, a shortish tail, and buck teeth. The animal looked like a beaver, but without the big, flat tail.

Vic gasped. "A woodchuck!"

"Joe hasn't been the only one eating the edible landscape behind my back. Woody's the reason we're out of the running for the FEEL Contest." Frank flicked a string bean on one of the too-short vines climbing up the fence. "My green bean plants were nearly as tall as your cucumbers before Woody and his friends started gnawing on them."

"Turns out woodchucks don't chuck wood at all," Joe said. "They chuck Frank's beans!"

"They're also called groundhogs, and now I know why," Frank added with a sigh. "They hog all the veggies. They like green beans and just about everything else except for some of the herbs. Thanks to the woodchucks, my dreams of winning the contest are gone—along with most of my lettuce! They ate half the garden before we put up my WDS to keep them out."

"Your WD-what?" Vic asked.

"Woodchuck Defense System." Frank tapped the white picket fence Vic was leaning on. "Two layers. Cedar wood on the front so it looks nice, with impenetrable wire fencing on the back so nothing can slip or chew through."

Vic gave a tug on the sturdy steel wire. The metal seemed too thick to gnaw through, and the holes in the wire fence were only about two inches wide.

Woody barely seemed to notice them as he walked over to the far corner of the fence and jammed his nose into a large bowl filled with old fruit. A second later, he stood up on his hind legs, holding an apple core between paws that looked like little gloved hands, and started to stuff his face.

"You guys are feeding them?!" Vic asked.

"*Joe* is feeding them," Frank corrected.

Joe shrugged. "Woody and his friends are cute. And I feel bad about locking him out of the garden. It's not his fault Frank grows such tasty veggies." Joe popped a ripe red cherry tomato into his mouth.

Frank sighed again. "Thankfully, groundhogs seem to like old fruit even more than vegetables."

"Bananas are Woody's favorite," Joe added.

"And if we feed them, they'll be less tempted to steal anything from someone else's garden," Frank

explained. "There's no way they're getting through my WDS either way."

"Now you just need to build a fence to keep Joe out," Vic said.

Joe grinned and chomped down on another tomato. Frank threw up his hands.

"I sure am glad I don't have any furry frenemies on my side of the street. I don't know what I'd do if something tried to eat my veggies." Vic paused. "We have a mouse in our house, but that doesn't bother me. It drives my parents bananas, though. Mice can flatten their bodies like little furry pancakes to squeeze through teeny-tiny cracks, so they're really hard to keep out. On the plus side for me, they're happier in the pantry than the garden."

"You might not know from looking at them, but mice and woodchucks are related," Frank said. "Groundhogs aren't really hogs at all. They're rodents. Just supersize ones that like to eat fruits and vegetables instead of cheese."

Vic laughed. "Good thing my parents don't need to worry about woodchucks in the house."

DING! DING!

Frank, Joe, and Vic all looked up at the sound of a bike bell approaching. The dinging wasn't coming from a bike, though. There was a giant pickle barreling down the street toward them!

The pickle was on top of a cart being pulled by a green electric scooter, ridden by a girl about their age.

"The Pickle Palace!" Joe hopped up and jogged over to the fence as the girl pulled her vehicle to a stop. The pickle cart was big enough for a kid to climb inside and had windows cut into it. THE PICKLE PRINCESS'S PICKLE PALACE was painted on both sides in large purple letters.

"Hey, Violet," Frank said. "How's the pickle cart business?"

The girl adjusted her purple-framed glasses and jumped off her scooter. "Business is booming. Everyone likes a cool pickle on a hot summer day."

"Count me in!" Joe said, pulling a few crumpled bills from his pocket. "I'll take two."

"What flavors? I've got five varieties today." She pointed to the chalkboard menu hanging next to the window. "I've also got pickled hot peppers, kimchi, and kraut."

"I'll take a Kosher Classic with extra dill and a Hot-Hot-Hot-Hot House." Joe gave the menu another glance. "You can throw in a cup of Red, White, and You multicolored kraut too."

"Coming right up!" Violet opened a door in the back of the pickle cart and climbed inside. She appeared at the window a moment later with a tray. Joe slapped a couple bills next to it and started chowing down.

"The garden's looking good, boys," Violet said, taking in the Hardys' edible front yard.

"Not good enough to win the FEEL Contest," Frank said, frowning again.

"Who cares about silly contests?" Violet took a bite of one of her own hot peppers. "I'm too busy with the Pickle Palace to waste time trying to make my garden look pretty for some judge. *Whoo!* That's spicy!"

"I can't believe you're not even going to try," Vic said. "I mean, it's going to be hard to beat me, but they're giving out awards for runners-up in different categories too."

"Eh. I've got my eyes on a bigger pr—" Violet

stopped talking, her mouth hanging open, as she stared through the pickle cart's other window at Vic's front yard across the street. "Prize. Wow, Vic! Your cucumbers are amazing!"

Vic smiled proudly. "The best in Bayport."

Violet whistled. "I bet they'd make some tasty pickles."

"They're way too pretty to pick or pickle," Vic replied. "Those beauties aren't going anywhere until the contest is over and I've been crowned champion."

Violet shook her head. "What good is growing food if you can't pickle and eat it?"

"ThatsmoreorlesswhatIsaid!" Joe mumbled through a mouthful of sauerkraut.

"We can eat it *after* the contest," Frank said.

"Not everyone in Bayport has the feels for FEEL, you know," Violet said, stepping out of the Pickle Palace. "I just got back from my pickle cart rounds at the farmers' market, and a lot of the folks there aren't happy about the contest at all. Farmer Phil said it's stealing their customers."

Farmer Phil ran the largest produce stand at the farmers' market.

Vic rolled his eyes. "That's ridiculous. It's not like I'm selling my cucumbers."

"Nope, but not as many people need to buy their veggies from the market now that everyone is growing their own," Violet explained as she hopped back on her scooter.

Vic thought for a second. "I guess that's true. My parents used to shop at the market all the time, but now we grow exactly what we want right outside our front door. We planted extra of the things we like best, so we can pick some and still have some to display for the judges."

Violet revved her scooter's motor. "I've got more pickles to sell. I'll see you boys later."

"Thanks for the tasty snack!" Joe called after her.

"Pickle power!" she yelled as the Pickle Palace picked up speed and disappeared down the block.

"Speaking of Farmer Phil, Woody's fruit buffet is almost ready for a refill," Joe said, turning to Vic, who looked confused. "Phil gives us a discount on the overripe fruit he doesn't sell."

"That way, we can also help Farmer Phil reduce food waste, so the leftover produce doesn't just get thrown out," added Frank.

"I still can't believe you're feeding the woodch—" Vic didn't get a chance to finish his sentence.

Only it wasn't Frank or Joe who interrupted him. The brothers looked almost as stunned as Vic when a blast of water sent him flying off his feet.

EDIBLE ENVY

"Ahhhhhhhh!" Vic screamed as he landed on his backside.

The stream of water disappeared as suddenly as it had appeared, leaving Vic sitting soggily in a puddle on the sidewalk.

Frank and Joe heard a gasp from across the street, the same direction the water had come from. They looked up to see a girl standing wide-eyed on the second-floor balcony of the house next door to

Vic's. She wore a bright blue hijab. The headscarf was wrapped neatly around her neck and over the shoulder of her long, flowy dark-blue shirt. One hand covered the girl's mouth while the other held the nozzle of a long garden hose—a *really* long garden hose. It was so long, it had been pulled inside through an open first-floor window, and through the house, onto the second-floor balcony!

"Audrika!" Vic snarled.

She dropped the hose and ran back inside. A minute later, the front door of the house flew open and Audrika came bursting out, her scarf waving in the air behind her and her sneakers squeaking against the pavement as she ran across the street toward Vic. Joe noticed that the knees of her jeans were dirty, just like Frank's and Vic's.

"I'm so sorry, Vic! I didn't mean to spray you!" Audrika went to help him up, but he waved her away and climbed back to his feet on his own.

Joe looked at the first-floor window where the hose had been pulled inside from the front yard. "Did you really drag that hose all the way up the stairs to the balcony? That's what I call extreme gardening!"

"I was trying to get just the right angle to water my berry patch, but"—she looked away in embarrassment—"I must have accidentally turned the hose to full force. My brother, Amir, got me a new high-tech garden nozzle with twenty different settings. I'm still kind of getting the hang of it."

"An accident? Likely story," Vic said, trying to squeeze the water out of his shirt.

"Really, Vic! I wouldn't spray you on purpose." Audrika sounded genuinely hurt. "I'm just a little klutzy sometimes."

"It's true," Joe said. "In robotics class, she knocked over half the lab equipment trying to invent a walking weed puller."

Audrika rubbed her forehead. "That one really hurt."

"Um, are you sure it's safe for you to be watering from the balcony like that?" Frank asked, shaking off some of the water that had splattered on him. "Your garden is gorgeous, but I don't want you to fall taking care of it!"

Audrika didn't seem to notice Frank's concern, but she did beam at the compliment.

"Her garden is okay," Vic muttered.

"I don't know. I'd say first prize is a toss-up between the two of you. I mean, look at those sunflowers!" Joe whistled. "They're so big, they actually look like the sun."

The front of Audrika's edible lawn was lined with giant, twelve-foot-tall sunflowers. Behind those were neatly tended rows of purple cabbages the size of soccer balls, striped green watermelons as big as basketballs, and pepper plants in a variety of colors, shapes, and sizes.

Vic scowled. "Her sunflowers have nothing on my cucumbers."

"It's not a contest, Vic," Audrika said.

"Um, technically, it *is* a contest," replied Joe.

"Oh yeah." Audrika narrowed her eyes. "And I'm going to win! Besides, I don't even like cucumbers. I bet the judges won't either, not once they parade past my peppers."

"Your peppers are paltry in comparison to my passionflowers." Vic narrowed *his* eyes and pointed at the alien-looking purple pinwheel flowers and lime-size fruit climbing the fence across from his cucumbers.

"Yeah, well, your passionflowers are blah next to my bee balm and borage butterfly buffet!" Audrika stabbed her finger at a patch of tall flowers, some topped with fuzzy-looking purple, pink, and red pom-poms, others covered in small baby-blue stars. Bees and butterflies buzzed and fluttered all around the blooms.

"The butterflies like my coneflowers better than your boring borage!" Vic yelled.

"Whoa, hold up, you two!" Frank said, jumping between them. "This is supposed to be a friendly competition. You both worked really hard and have great gardens. You can both want to win the contest and still be friends."

"You're right, Frank." Audrika bit her lip and turned back to Vic. "You do have a very nice garden. And I really am sorry for spraying you."

Vic kicked at the ground without looking up. "Well, I guess you didn't mean to do it."

Audrika smiled. "I've got to finish my watering. I'll see you guys later."

She looked both ways, then jogged back across the street to her house.

Vic trudged back to his yard a moment later, mumbling to himself. "My garden is so much better than hers."

"Who knew gardening was such a competitive sport?" Joe said, munching on a mint leaf. "Ah, nature's mouthwash!"

That night Frank dreamed of bean plants so tall, they climbed through the clouds. Joe dreamed of skipping through an endless garden with a troupe of dancing woodchucks in top hats, eating all the yummy fruits and veggies as he went.

The sun was just starting to rise the next morning, and the Hardy boys were still asleep, when—

"AHHHHHHHHHHHHHH!"

A sound jolted the boys awake, and it wasn't their alarm clock.

It was a scream.

And it was coming from across the street!

CUCUMBER CRIME SCENE

They boys didn't bother wasting time getting dressed. They sprinted right outside in their pajamas.

"I thought I recognized that scream," Joe said as they raced across the street to Vic's house.

Vic was on his knees in his garden, looking up at his cucumber plants. As the boys got closer, they realized that Vic's glorious cukes weren't quite so glorious anymore. Half the vines were gone!

"My beautiful cucumbers," Vic moaned. "Someone sabotaged them!"

"Sabotage?" Frank echoed, taking in the scene.

"My cucumbers couldn't have done this to themselves." Vic's voice shook as he struggled to hold back tears.

Frank turned to Joe. "You know what that means."

Joe nodded. "A mystery."

"Did you bring it?" Frank asked.

"Yup." Joe held up a notebook. "I didn't bother putting on real pants, but I did grab the clue book. A scream at sunrise is usually a good sign we might need it."

"Clue book?" Vic asked.

"It's where we write down the five *W*s."

Vic gave Joe a confused look. "The five whats?"

"Just one *what*," Joe said. "The other four *W*s stand for *who*, *where*, *when*, and *why*."

"Those are the five questions we have to answer to solve any case," Frank explained. "Who did it? What did they do? Where did it happen? When did they do it? And why did they do it?"

"We know *what* and *where* already," Joe said as he wrote *cucumber sabotage* and *Vic's garden*.

Frank scanned the ground, trying to spot anything unusual. "We're going to have to dig deeper to get answers to the other *W*s."

Joe's stomach began to rumble as he sniffed the air. "Are those bananas I smell?"

"Let's focus on the case. You can get breakfast after we examine the crime scene." Frank bent over to get a closer look at the damaged plants. Some of the tall vines had been yanked off the bamboo trellis and lay limply on the ground with most of their leaves missing. Others had tattered stems that ended less than a foot off the ground. There were torn bits of vines, leaves, and cucumber pieces everywhere. "I don't see a pattern to the damage. It looks like someone just went down the row hacking and yanking wherever they felt like it."

"Whoever did this sure wasn't neat about it," Joe said, leaning over next to Frank.

"There are enough plants left that I can at least pretty them up for the judges before the contest ends." Vic started pulling the ruined vines out of the ground. "I'll have to throw the damaged plants in the compost pile, but I can transplant some of my edible flowers to fill the empty spaces."

Frank patted Vic on the shoulder. "That sounds

like a great plan. Your garden is still impressive, even without as many cucumbers."

"You can't count me out yet!" Vic shook his fist at the sky.

"I think that brings us to *why*," Frank said.

"I bet we're thinking the same thing, bro." Joe picked up a piece of vine. "Could someone have hacked down our man Vic's cukes to knock a top competitor out of the running for the FEEL Contest?"

Vic threw a nub of half-mashed cucumber to the ground. "Isn't it obvious that's what happened?"

"Something's weird about this damage," Frank said as he studied the ragged end of the vine he was holding. "The saboteur couldn't have used a regular knife or scissors. The cut would be cleaner."

Joe took the vine from him and tried tearing it in half with his hands. It was really hard to do! When the stem finally pulled apart, the ends were a lot more bent and stringy than the sabotaged one. He held the two pieces up for Frank and Vic to see. "It doesn't look like they used their hands, either."

Frank crouched down and picked up the cucumber nub Vic had tossed aside. The end was all lumpy with uneven marks all the way around the edges. Frank ground his teeth together. "You know what these look like?"

"Oh . . . ," Joe muttered.

"*Oh?*" Vic looked between Joe and Frank. "What does *oh* mean?"

"I don't think your vines were hacked or torn," Frank said. "They were chewed!"

"*Chewed?*" Vic repeated. "Who would do such a thing?"

Joe looked nervously down at his feet. "Um, I think we have our prime suspect."

"Wait, why do *you* look guilty?" Vic asked, eyeing Joe suspiciously.

Joe gulped. "I think the culprit might be a friend of mine."

Frank glared across the street at the Hardys' own garden. "Woody."

Chapter 5

FENCE DEFENSE!

"Your woodchuck ate my cucumbers?!" Vic yelled.

"Woody sure isn't my woodchuck." Frank threw his hands up in the air. "It could have been one of his relatives. He's not the only one in the neighborhood."

Joe smile nervously. "Normally, we'd confront the suspect, but it's not like we can interrogate Woody and his friends."

"We may not be able to talk to them, but I

do know how to keep them from doing it again," Frank said.

"Your WDS!" Joe declared.

"Yes! A fence! I'll have my mom go to the hardware store to pick up the supplies," Vic called over his shoulder as he sprinted toward the house. The brothers followed.

After Frank gave Mrs. Blake a list of what to get, the boys changed into their gardening clothes. A few hours later, the three were hard at work putting up a Woodchuck Defense System fence around Vic's garden.

"We have to dig down and put the wire fence a whole foot underground, so the critters don't get any ideas about trying to dig under it," Frank explained, grabbing a shovel. "Remember when I told you woodchucks are also called groundhogs because they hog all the veggies? Well, there's another reason. They're experts at digging holes and underground tunnels."

A few minutes later Audrika came outside. "Whoa, what are you guys doing?"

Joe chuckled. "You mean Vic's scream didn't wake you earlier?"

"I'm a heavy sleeper. My brother says I can sleep through just about anything." Her mouth dropped open when she noticed Vic's half-eaten cucumber plants. "What happened to your garden?"

Vic angrily stabbed a fence post into the ground. "Woodchucks."

By the time the boys finished telling Audrika the whole story, she looked horrified. "What if the woodchucks attack my garden next?" She eyed her family's fenceless yard. "I need a WDS too!"

"We can help you build one when we're done over here," Frank offered.

Joe handed Audrika a hammer. "With four of us working together, we can get them both done in no time."

Frank smiled as Audrika started pounding down a post. "See? You can be competitors *and* teammates."

"Woodchucks won't be bothering either of you anymore," Frank said a few hours later when the final nail had been pounded.

DING! DING!

"Those are some fancy new fences you all have," Violet said, pulling the Pickle Palace to a stop in front of Audrika's house.

"We built them together," Audrika proudly replied.

"Wow, look at those peppers! And that cabbage!" Violet was practically drooling over the produce in Audrika's garden.

"The best on the block," Audrika said, flipping her hammer in the air and trying to catch it.

Only she missed.

"OUCH!" Vic screamed.

"Oops! Sorry!"

Vic glared up at her as he took off his boot and rubbed his foot. "It's a good thing I'm wearing my gardening boots, or you might have broken my toe."

"Speaking of broken . . ." Violet whistled. "What happened to your cucumbers?"

Vic groaned.

"A woodchuck got them," explained Frank.

"What a shame. All those cukes will never grow up to be tasty pickles." Violet shook her head sadly. "Well, I gotta go," she said after a moment. "The people need their pickles!"

"There's one more thing we need to do," Joe said as the Pickle Palace drove away. "The WDSs should protect the two of you, but we should look out for the rest of our neighbors. If we put more fruit out, it will help keep the woodchucks happy so they won't have to break into anyone else's yards."

"Good call, Joe." Frank gave his brother a pat on the back. "I think a trip to the farmers' market is in order."

After grabbing their bikes, the Hardys invited the others to come, but Audrika said she was going to hang back to clean up the construction site, and Vic wanted to tend to his wounded cucumbers.

"There's Violet's house," Joe said when they reached the end of the block.

"I can smell it from here." Frank inhaled deeply. "Oregano. Rosemary. Is that thyme?"

Joe sniffed. "And dill! You can practically taste the pickles!"

The boys pulled to a stop in front of the house. Violet's family had an edible garden as well, but unlike the other neighbors' neatly tended yards, the Parkers' was totally wild-looking and overgrown.

"It's like an herb jungle," Frank said. "I've never seen so many different types in one place."

Some plants grew in sprawling bushes, some in tall stalks. Some were planted in the ground, some sprouted from clay pots and apple boxes and even an old bathtub. Others crept all over the place, spilling onto the walk or poking up through cracks in the stone.

"If there's a FEEL award for the messiest garden, I think Violet has it in the bag," Joe quipped.

Frank leaned down to pluck a dandelion from the edge of the yard. "She did say she didn't care about the contest."

Joe took another deep breath. "There are herbs everywhere, but I don't see any veggies. I wonder where she gets all the stuff she pickles."

Frank shrugged and started pedaling again. "Speaking of getting stuff, let's go pick up that woodchuck fruit before the critters strike again."

"Violet was right," Frank said as they pulled up to the not-so-crowded Bayport Farmers' Market. "The stalls don't look as busy as they usually do."

There were stands for all kinds of produce, baked

goods, and crafts. The biggest tent had a sign out front that read FARMER PHIL'S FARM-FRESH FOOD—GROWING OUR COMMUNITY. Crates overflowed with fruits and veggies. A tall, lanky man sat on a barrel behind the folding tables wearing faded blue jeans, a plaid shirt, and a ball cap with a smiling cartoon carrot on it.

"Hey, boys," he called.

"Hi, Farmer Phil!" Joe waved, pulling his bike to a stop. "We're here for a fruit refill."

"Well, you're in luck. I've got extra for you that I'll throw in for free. Unfortunately, my produce isn't selling like it used to."

"We heard business was down because of the FEEL Contest," Frank said.

"Yeah, I'm not really feeling it." Phil wiggled his bushy eyebrows.

Joe laughed. "Wow, that pun was almost as bad as one of Frank's."

"Sales are down, but I'm not too worried," Phil said, tossing an onion up in the air and catching it. "I bet my old customers will be back in no time. People will get bored of growing their own food once the contest is over and there aren't any more prizes to win. I sure do appreciate you boys helping me out, though. And the environment." He picked up an overflowing bin of assorted fruit. Some of it was overripe, but most of it was still edible, even for a non-woodchuck. "I don't want to haul this back to the compost bin on the farm, and I definitely don't want to throw it out. Way too much uneaten food gets wasted or ends up in landfills already."

Phil pointed to a hand-painted sign behind the counter:

FARMER PHIL'S *PHIL*OSOPHY
LET'S GROW OUR COMMUNITY
TOGETHER
EAT LOCAL • PICK FRESH
WASTE LESS • ENJOY MORE
SUSTAINABLE FOOD & FRIENDSHIP

Joe took the bin of fruit from Farmer Phil while Frank pulled out a few dollars to pay.

"Well, thanks for the extra leftovers. We can sure use them. The woodchucks we told you about are attacking our neighbors' gardens now. We put up more fencing, but these goodies should keep the critters from sneaking snacks they're not supposed to."

"Those 'chucks sure can be pesky," Phil said, tidying up the onion bin. "It's awfully nice of you boys to give them a free meal instead of just shooing them off."

"Woody and his pals are too cute to chase away,"

Joe said, strapping the fruit bin to the back of his bike. "No bananas?"

"I only get a few at a time from my friend's greenhouse. Gotta save the hard-to-grow specialty items for my customers, and I know you said your 'chucks like them nice and ripe. This batch is still green."

"That's okay," Joe said. "There are more than enough yummy goodies here to keep them happy."

"Good luck, boys!" Phil called as the brothers rode away.

Frank waved back. "Thanks, Farmer Phil!"

By the time they got back to their block, Vic had almost finished replacing the damaged cucumber plants with an eye-popping mix of red and yellow marigolds. His garden wasn't the cucumber paradise it had been, but it was still impressive. And a few minutes later, there was a new woodchuck buffet set up outside Vic's fence to help keep it that way.

"That was a successful day of detecting and protecting," Joe said as the boys brushed their teeth before bed that night.

"Yup." Frank said through a gurgle. "We identified the suspect and helped save our neighbors' gardens in time for the contest."

"And kept Woody and his woodchuck friends happy at the same time."

"I'd say it's case closed."

"Eyes closed too!" said Joe. "Good night, bro!"

The boys barely noticed the crashing thunder and pouring rain outside as they fell asleep.

The next morning the sun was just starting to rise, and they were still asleep when—

"AHHHHHHHHHHHHHH! NOT AGAIN!"

Chapter 6

NEFARIOUS NEIGHBORLINESS

The boys ran across the street in their pajamas (again!) to find Vic on his knees (again!) staring at his cucumber plants (again!). Only this time, there were almost none of them left.

"The woodchucks came back!" Vic wailed.

The damage was like the day before, just worse. There were more gnawed and tattered pieces of vine, more bits of leaves, and more chunks of cucumbers everywhere.

"It's total cucumber carnage," Joe whispered.

"But how?" Frank stared at the brand-new double-layer fence around Vic's yard. "We put up the WDS."

Vic pointed at Frank. "Your fence is a failure!" He moved his finger to Joe. "And your woodchucks are weasels!"

"We followed my blueprints exactly. The WDS has to be secure." Frank gave the fence a shake. It seemed as sturdy as ever.

"And I was sure the fruit buffet would keep them happy." Joe examined a piece of chewed-up vine. "This does look like another groundhog heist, though."

He went over to the fence and eyed the bin of fruit he'd set up a safe distance away on the other side. Some of it had been eaten by the woodchucks, but not that much. He stared at the muddy ground.

"Hmm . . ." Joe grabbed the top of the fence, lifted himself up, and climbed over.

Frank hurried to get a closer look; he couldn't tell what Joe had seen, but he knew from his brother's expression that it was probably a clue.

Joe pointed to prints in the mud. "Look at those thin-fingered paws with pointy nails. These are definitely woodchuck tracks. They aren't the only ones, though."

Frank hopped over the fence and leaned down to study the ground where the mud was streaked beneath the paw prints. "Huh. It looks like someone brushed over the mud with something before the woodchuck stepped in the same spot."

"Almost like they were trying to cover up a different kind of track." Joe drew an air circle over a curved dent in the mud. "That looks like it could be part of a heel print from someone's shoe."

Frank frowned. "If it is, it's too smudged to tell how big the foot was."

"You mean someone tried to cover up their footprints?" Vic asked.

Joe nodded. "Like a bigger, human pest tried to make it look like a woodchuck did the damage."

Vic gasped. "A person did this?"

"It's possible," Frank said. "The clues don't totally add up. Those are definitely woodchuck tracks, but something about these marks smells fishy. And by fishy, I mean human-y."

"Audrika," Vic snarled.

Frank held up his hand. "It's never good to accuse someone of a crime without evidence. Just because you two are rivals doesn't make her a prime suspect."

Vic scowled at the house next door. "No, but her sneaking out of her house late last night does."

⇆ 47

"She what?" Frank and Joe asked at the same time.

Vic turned back to the brothers. "The thunder woke me up. I meant to go right back to sleep, but I had an idea about a new pruning technique that would make my tomato plants look perfect before the competition, so I went to grab my garden journal. It's kind of like your clue book, just for gardening notes instead of mysteries. Anyway, that's when I looked out the window and saw it: Audrika wearing a raincoat, running out her back door into the storm."

Frank and Joe exchanged a look.

"I figured maybe she was checking on her sunflowers to make sure they didn't get blown over," Vic continued, "but now I know what she was really doing. Sabotage!"

Joe pulled out the clue book. "I hate to admit it, but Audrika does have a *why*."

"To win," Frank finished as Joe wrote down the latest information. "We don't know the exact time Vic's cukes were victimized, but it had to be overnight."

"She was in the vicinity of the crime scene *when* the crime took place. Vic saw her," Joe said, making another note.

Vic threw down the half-eaten cucumber he was holding and started marching toward Audrika's house. "I'm not letting her get away with this!"

"Hold on," Frank said, putting a hand on Vic's shoulder. "Why don't you clean up your garden while Joe and I talk to Audrika?"

"Yeah," Joe chimed in. "After all, we still don't have proof that she did anything, and my bro and I are trained in interrogating suspects."

Vic shot one last glare at Audrika's house, then turned back to his plants.

Frank and Joe knocked on Audrika's door. Her brother Amir answered. He was a couple of years older than Audrika and was wearing a paper party crown that looked like a birthday cake with candles sticking up.

"Hey, guys! Did you come to wish me happy birthday?" he asked.

"Nope," Joe said. "Happy birthday, though!"

"Happy birthday, Amir," Frank added. "Is your sister around?"

"Hi, Hardys, what's up?" Audrika said before Amir could reply.

"More like what's down," quipped Joe.

Audrika seemed confused.

"Down. As in Vic's cucumbers," Frank explained.

"His cucumbers?" Audrika stepped out onto the porch and took in Vic's garden destruction. "The woodchucks struck again?!"

"Or someone," Frank said, crossing his arms.

"Wait, why are you looking at me like that?" Audrika asked.

"Vic saw you sneaking out late last night," replied Frank.

"You snuck out of the house?" Amir's eyes went wide.

"In the middle of a storm," Joe added.

"You know we're not allowed outside at night!"

"I didn't, uh . . . I mean, it's just, I—" Audrika fumbled while Frank, Joe, and Amir all waited. "I didn't sneak out. I just—I left something in the garden. Some, uh, seeds. I didn't want them to get ruined in the rain."

"You didn't go anywhere else?" her brother asked.

Audrika shook her head. She had started to turn red.

"Like, say, the garden next door?" Joe suggested.

"No! I didn't go anywhere, but, um—" She looked nervously at her brother. "Just our garden to get the tools, so they wouldn't, um, rust."

Frank leaned in. "I thought you said you left your seeds."

"Seeds!" She nodded so fast, it looked like she might hurt herself. "And tools! Just seeds and tools!" Her voice cracked, and she wouldn't meet anyone's eye.

"Then how do you explain—" Before Frank could finish his question, Mrs. Khaleel's voice called from the house.

"Amir! Audrika! Come! Your grandmother is video-chatting to say happy birthday!"

"Nanu!" Amir yelled, running inside.

"Bye!" Audrika squeaked, then slammed the door in Frank's and Joe's faces.

"Well, that was suspicious," Joe said. "She was squirming like a garden worm."

Frank eyed the door. "She couldn't keep her story straight. No one flip-flops on an alibi like that unless they're hiding something."

"I think I know what we'll be doing later."

Frank looked back across the street at their own house. Joe's bedroom window had a clear view of Audrika's and Vic's gardens. "Stakeout time."

"We can watch and see if the perp strikes again," Joe suggested as they crossed the street back to their yard. "If the cucumber crusher is Audrika, we'll catch her in the act."

"This will be the perfect spot to watch both Audrika's house and Vic's garden," Joe said later that day, setting a pair of binoculars and the clue book beside his bedroom window.

Frank peeked out through the curtains. "Once the sun goes down, we can take turns to make sure we don't miss anything. Until then, we should stay away from the window, so no one sees us and gets suspicious."

"I know the perfect way to pass the time," Joe said. "Food!"

They were in the kitchen, discussing their stake-out plans over a plate of cheese sandwiches with cherry tomatoes from the garden, when—

"AHHHHHHHHHHHHHH!" Another scream reached them from across the street.

But this time it wasn't Vic.

It was Audrika!

Chapter 7

MOUSE MANEUVERS

Frank and Joe ran across the street for the third time in two days. Audrika was on the ground, wailing in front of her tattered vegetables.

"My peppers are pulverized!" she cried. "My cabbages are kaput!"

Half of Audrika's once-perfect soccer-ball-size cabbages had been gnawed to bits. There were pieces of purple and white cabbage everywhere, almost like the vegetables had exploded. Her magnificent

multicolored peppers hadn't escaped the massacre.
Some of them were chewed off right down to the
bottoms of the stems.

"I didn't see this twist coming," said Joe, sizing
up the mess.

Frank turned his attention back to Audrika.
"What happened?"

"I came out to check on my veggies, and they were
just—" She picked up a hunk of cabbage covered

with tooth marks. "All that hard work—gone!"

Joe sighed. "So is our entire theory of the case."

"You guys didn't really think I would ruin Vic's cucumbers, did you?"

"Well—" Frank looked away. "You did have a motive, and you were acting pretty suspicious when we asked you about why you'd snuck out last night. But it doesn't make any sense for you to be a victim *and* the villain."

"Unless you really did sabotage Vic's garden and were trying to make it seem like you were attacked too, so we wouldn't suspect you," Joe suggested, flipping open the clue book.

Audrika jumped to her feet and put her hands on her hips. "You think I'd destroy my own garden? And sink my chances of winning the contest?"

"Yeah, it's not a very good theory," Frank agreed.

"Unless Vic attacked your garden to get back at you, and you're both guilty," Joe said.

Audrika growled.

"Sorry," Joe added quickly. "I'm not accusing you. It's just that there's something strange going on, and we have to consider all the possibilities so we can cross the ones that don't fit off our list."

"So you think Vic could have done this?" she asked, eyeing her next-door neighbor's house.

Joe wrote Vic's name under *Suspects*. "He thinks you might have destroyed his garden. He could have wanted revenge."

"I don't know, Joe." Frank looked around at the damage. "This really appears to be a woodchuck attack. Whatever attacked Vic's garden seems to have struck Audrika's garden too."

"Let's examine the crime scene more closely—" A rustling sound over by the collard greens in the corner of the garden interrupted Joe's thought.

"I don't think we're alone." Frank stalked toward the collard greens.

A furry brown head popped up between the plants and met his gaze, a leaf still dangling from its bucktoothed mouth.

Frank gasped. "The perp is still here!"

Joe buried his face in his hands. "And it *is* a woodchuck!"

Frank threw his arms up. "But how does it keep getting past my Woodchuck Defense System?"

Audrika shouted as she ran at the collard green thief. "Go away, woodchuck! You're not welcome here!"

"He's making a run for it!" Joe called out as the woodchuck bolted from the collards toward the fence, its round belly almost touching the ground.

"It's cornered. There's no way it's going to be able to get out of—" Frank's mouth dropped open.

Audrika gasped.

Joe blinked his eyes rapidly. He couldn't believe what he was seeing.

The chubby fur ball dove headfirst for the fence—and somehow squeezed its oversize rodent body right through one of the tiny, two-inch squares in the metal wire, popped out the other side, puffed back up to its normal size, and waddled to freedom.

"It—it—" Audrika was too stunned to finish her sentence.

"Shrank," Joe said.

"Like magic," Audrika whispered.

"Not like magic," Frank said. "Like a giant mouse!"

Chapter 8

WHY DID THE WOODCHUCK CROSS THE ROAD?

Frank, Joe, and Audrika watched in disbelief as the woodchuck dashed across the street and disappeared.

"I guess the case is solved," Joe said, sounding a lot sadder than he usually did when they cracked a case. "A woodchuck really did do it. But they're so cute. I feel betrayed."

"I guess my Woodchuck Defense System isn't as impenetrable as I thought." Frank kicked at one of the posts. "That one wasn't as big as Woody, but I still didn't expect the critters to be able to squeeze their bodies together like that."

"You're the one who told us groundhogs weren't really hogs," Joe pointed out.

Frank hung his head. "They're relatives of the mice that slip through the cracks in Vic's house." He turned to Audrika. "I'm sorry my defense system failed you."

"It's not your fault," she said. "You guys did your best. That woodchuck was like a magician. An *evil* magician."

Joe scratched his nose. "I'm sorry too, Audrika. I kept defending the woodchucks, but Woody's friends were guilty the whole time."

Frank got down on his knees and studied the two-inch-square opening where the woodchuck had escaped. He plucked a piece of brown fur from the metal wire. "Something is still weird about this whole thing. If the woodchucks could squeeze through the fence this whole time, why did the hungry hogs leave our garden alone after we put up our WDS?"

"That's a good point," Joe said. "This woodchuck

was smaller than Woody, but we've seen even smaller woodchucks around, and they never snuck through our fence."

"So my defense system may not be foolproof, but it does discourage them." Frank held up the hunk of fur. "That incredible shrinking 'chuck act was impressive, but it couldn't have been comfortable."

"And there are plenty of yummy treats in the fruit buffet to keep them happy without losing any fur," Joe said.

Frank scratched his head. "So why did the woodchuck ignore our fence and pass up all that free fruit to break into your and Vic's gardens? Especially when they didn't bother all our neighbors who don't even have fences around their gardens?"

Audrika shrugged. "You guys are the detectives."

A summer breeze whooshed through the garden, rustling the leaves of the oregano bush in the other corner and making the sunflowers sway.

Joe sniffed the air. "What's that?"

"What's what?" Frank asked.

Joe sniffed again, following his nose back across the garden. "Bananas. Rotten bananas. I smelled them the first time Vic's garden was attacked." He got down on his knees by what was left of the cabbage patch, dipped his finger in something brownish and mushy, and held it up to eye level. "Banana bits!"

"Banana bits?" Audrika echoed.

"Banana bits!" Frank ran to join Joe. "One of woodchucks' favorite foods."

"But I'm not growing bananas—" Audrika began.

"Exactly!" Frank said.

There was another lump of mashed banana a few feet away. And another a few feet from that.

"This one has a woodchuck paw print in it!" Joe said.

The trio followed the banana trail across the garden to the oregano bush. Tall, thin, leafy green stems led to clusters of tiny pink and purple flowers. The plant had a strong, spicy aroma, but not so spicy that they couldn't still smell the unmistakable scent of overripe banana.

Joe pushed aside the herb stalks. "The fence is totally smeared with banana!"

That wasn't the most surprising part, though.

There was a woodchuck-size hole cut in the wire!

Chapter 9

PICK A PECK OF
UN-PICKLED PEPPERS

"That woodchuck may have escaped by squeezing through the fence wire after we cornered it, but I don't think that's how it got in." Joe pushed his entire arm through the hole and moved it around. "This is."

"Someone sabotaged my Woodchuck Defense System!" Frank cried.

"And my garden!" Audrika stomped on a bit of mushed banana.

"And mine!" Vic yelled, sprinting over from next door. "I was watching from the kitchen window, but my parents wouldn't let me come out until I finished the dishes." He paused to study the hole for himself. "A secret groundhog entrance."

"I bet the groundhog would have exited that way too if we hadn't been blocking its path," Joe said. "We scared the poor thing, and it needed a quick way out."

Frank carefully ran his fingers along the edge of the hole. "You can see where someone snipped the fence with wire cutters to make it easy for the critter to mosey right in."

"Then they lured it with groundhogs' favorite grub," Audrika said, pounding her fist into her palm.

"The woodchuck is the fall guy!" Joe declared.

"I bet if we look closely enough, we'll find a hole cut in Vic's fence too," Frank said.

The four went next door to Vic's garden, and sure enough, there was another neatly snipped hole hidden behind the coneflowers.

"We might have discovered it sooner if there

hadn't been that big storm," Joe said. "The rain must have washed away the smell of the banana bait. I have a finely tuned food sniffer, but that was a doozy of a downpour."

"You smelled banana the first time the woodchuck attacked my garden," Vic said. "Before we put up the fence."

Frank tapped his nose. "My brother, the human hound dog."

"Forget hound dogs. What are we going to do about the groundhogs?" Audrika demanded. "The block party is tomorrow! The whole garden could get eaten before the judges even get to see it!"

"Well, I can repair the Woodchuck Defense Systems in no time. The bigger question is, who cut the holes?"

"I'm happy Woody and his friends are off the hook," Joe said, "but we still don't know who framed them."

Vic eyed Audrika. "Are we sure she didn't do it and just sabotage herself so you wouldn't suspect her? She was super jealous of my clearly superior garden."

"Ha! My garden is clearly the superior one. It's too bad you can't admit it," Audrika shot back.

Joe cleared his throat loudly and opened the clue book. "I want to cross Audrika's name off the *who* list for good—" His cheeks turned red as he glanced up at her. "But you were acting really suspicious before when we asked you about it."

"Um, yeah, about that—" Audrika fiddled with her hands. "I do have a confession to make. I'm sorry I lied to you about why I snuck out of the house during the storm."

"I knew it!" Vic shouted.

"It wasn't to mess with your overgrown weed patch! I was going to Violet's house to buy an edible pickle arrangement for my brother's birthday."

Vic thrust a finger up in the air. "I knew—Wait, you what?"

"I would have told Frank and Joe when they asked me, but Amir was standing there, and I didn't want to ruin the surprise," she explained. "He really loves pickles, and I knew he'd be super excited when he got it."

Audrika pointed to her dining room window. Through it, the boys could see Amir happily chowing down on a huge plate of pickles arranged in the shape of a giant flower.

"I'd call that a credible edible alibi," Frank said.

"I know lying is wrong, though. I feel really bad about not being honest with you guys."

Vic shuffled from foot to foot. "Um, I think I'm the one who needs to say sorry. It was wrong to accuse you of framing the woodchucks and sabotaging our gardens."

"It's okay, Vic." Audrika gave him a small smile. "I think we both just love our gardens and were really upset. Still friends?"

Vic nodded shyly.

"Friends, and definitely not suspects," Joe said, crossing Audrika's and Vic's names off his clue book list.

Frank was still watching Amir eating his pickles. "Crew, I think we left a suspect off our list."

Audrika took a step backward. "You mean my brother?!"

"No," Frank said. "His pickle supplier."

"Violet!" Joe quickly wrote her name below Audrika's crossed-out one. "The Pickle Princess definitely has a motive."

"She needs cucumbers to make her pickles," said Vic.

"And peppers for her pickled peppers, and cabbage for her kimchi and kraut!" Audrika added.

Frank returned his focus to his friends. "When we rode by Violet's garden yesterday, there weren't *any* vegetables growing. Just herbs."

"And didn't she say how tasty pickles made from Vic's cukes would be?" asked Joe.

"It has to be her!" Vic and Audrika said at the same time.

"Audrika!" Mrs. Khaleel called from the front door. "Time to come in!"

"Gotta go, guys," Audrika said, running inside. "Coming, Ma!"

Vic sighed. "I have to go too. It's almost dinnertime, and then I've got to get my rest. I'm getting up extra early to put the final touches on my garden before the block party starts. I still haven't given up, even without my cucumbers."

"I think I can smell our dinner cooking too," Joe said. "And we'll also be getting up extra early, but not to garden."

Frank looked down the street. "We have a new suspect to interrogate, and we want to catch her before she starts her Pickle Palace rounds."

Frank and Joe hopped on their bikes early the next morning and headed for Violet's house. All down the street, neighbors were already outside getting ready for the block party. People were tidying their gardens, bringing out tables, and unpacking equipment from trucks.

When the brothers pedaled up to Violet's overgrown herb garden, she was out front loading the day's pickles into the back of the Pickle Palace.

"Hey, boys!" she called as they brought their bikes to a stop. "Big day today. I have a feeling the block party will help me break my pickle sales record."

"Yeah, but are they yours to sell?" Joe demanded.

"What do you mean?"

Frank crossed his arms. "Pickle profiteering."

"What's 'profiteering' mean?" Violet asked, appearing genuinely confused.

"To make money and profits illegally," Frank explained.

"Hey, man, my pickles are pure!" Violet pushed her purple-framed glasses back up her nose with one index finger and jabbed the other at Frank.

"Purely *pilfered*, maybe," Frank replied.

"What does 'pilfered' mean?" Joe whispered.

"Stolen," explained Frank.

"Stolen?! The Pickle Princess doesn't steal! I make all my pickles myself!"

"You might pickle them yourself, but where do you get the veggies?" Joe asked, glancing at her garden. "You've got a huge garden, but there's something missing."

"I see parsley, sage, rosemary, thyme, and about fifty other herbs and spices, but I don't see a single cucumber," Frank said.

"Or pepper or cabbage," added Joe.

"Vic and Audrika had tons of them, though," Frank said. "We saw you admiring their crops."

"Then someone sabotaged them and made it look like a woodchuck did all the damage," said Joe.

Violet blinked a few times. "And you think it was me?"

"You could have let the woodchucks eat enough of their vegetables to make it look like they were responsible, while you were busy stealing most of the harvest to turn into pickles," Joe said.

Frank tapped a knuckle on the pickle cart. "Once they're pickled, there'd be no way to trace where the veggies came from."

"We know where they *didn't* come from, though," Joe said. "Your garden."

Violet grinned. "Oh, no? You know outside isn't the only place you can have a garden, right?"

"Um . . ." Frank was suddenly feeling a lot less certain about his theory.

Violet shook her head and sighed, then started walking back toward her front door. "Follow me."

Frank and Joe trailed her through the overgrown

garden, past her front door, and down a set of steep, narrow stairs to the basement.

"I don't need to steal anyone else's veggies because I'm growing my own," Violet proclaimed. "Just not in my yard where the woodchucks can get to them." She pushed open a door at the bottom of the stairs.

"Welcome to my Pickle Bunker."

Frank and Joe gasped.

"It's beautiful," Frank whispered.

"Yup!" Violet agreed. "Three hundred square feet of homegrown cucumbers and peppers using indoor grow lights and a timed watering system of my own design."

The whole basement was filled with plants. The boys could practically taste the cucumber in the air.

"Uh, I guess this explains why you don't have any veggies in your front yard," Joe mumbled.

"The front yard is for my pickling herbs, and they grow like wild on their own. The critters don't like them much, the plants aren't too picky about how much water they get, and they're mostly perennials, so they come back every year. Cukes and peppers are more high maintenance, and they're annuals. They die when the weather gets cold, so you have to plant more in the spring. But not down here!" She opened her arms, gesturing to the plants all around her. "It's a perfectly controlled environment where my pickles-to-be can prosper. No pests, no bad weather, and one hundred percent absolutely no sabotage."

It was true. Violet had cucumbers and peppers to spare.

"You don't have a reason to steal anyone else's vegetables," Joe admitted.

"Sure don't!" Violet said. "And anytime I want a different variety of cucumbers or need to pick up cabbages for my kraut and kimchi, I just hit up the farmers' market. Prices are way down now that everyone's growing their own veggies, so I can get everything I need cheap. The farmers give me a great wholesale discount."

"And you don't care about the contest, so winning FEEL isn't a motive either," Frank said with a sigh.

"And without a *why*"—Joe crossed Violet's name off the clue book list—"we're back to square one."

"Sorry, boys. You're going to have to find a new suspect." Violet looked up at a clock on the wall. The minute and second hands were both shaped like pickles. "Time for me to run. Some of the farmers are so desperate to get rid of their extra produce, they'll even trade me veggies for free pickles. I'm going to drop some off now in exchange for some free fruit to munch on while I do my rounds."

Joe gave his pen a click. "Did you say free fruit?"

"Yup. Gotta keep my energy up for a long day of pickle selling. I'm planning to turn this block party into Pickle-Palooza!"

"Fruit, like maybe bananas?" Joe asked, suddenly more energetic.

Violet shrugged. "Sure, I like bananas."

"You can worry about your stomach later, Joe," Frank said, pulling his brother toward the door. "The contest is about to start, and we aren't any closer to solving the case than we were before."

"It's not *my* stomach I'm thinking about," Joe said. "Do you know what else likes free bananas?"

Frank thought for a second. "Woodchucks, but—"

Joe was yanking Frank up the basement stairs before he could finish his sentence. "Thanks, Violet! I think you gave us just the clue we needed!"

THE HARDY BOYS—and
YOU!

DO YOU KNOW WHO SABOTAGED AUDRIKA'S AND VIC'S
gardens? Think like a Hardy Boy and try cracking the case. Write your answers down on a piece of paper. Or just turn the page to find out!

1. Frank and Joe ruled out Audrika and Violet as suspects. Who else might have a reason to cut holes in the fences to let the woodchucks in? Write your answer down.

2. When Violet said she was going to trade her pickles for free fruit, Joe thought of a new clue. Can you think of any clues the boys might have missed the first time? Write your answer down.

3. Frank, Joe, and their neighbors are excited about growing their own food at home because it's tasty and good for the planet. Can you think of foods you like to eat that you might try growing in your own garden or in a pot on a sunny windowsill?

Chapter 10

THE GOOD, THE BAD, AND THE BANANAS

"Let's go!" Joe said, hopping on his bike.

"Go where?" Frank asked, scrambling onto his own bike and pedaling hard to catch up with his brother, who was already a block ahead.

"To the source!" Joe called back. "The banana source!"

"I know bananas are a clue, but what does that tell us that we don't know already?" Frank asked, finally coming up beside Joe. "Everyone can get bananas if they want them. Anyone could have used them as bait."

"Sure, but not everyone knows enough about woodchucks to know that mushy bananas are one of their favorite foods," Joe explained. "It hit me when Violet said she was getting free fruit at the farmers' market. There's a *who* at the market we didn't add to our suspect list."

Frank grinned, pedaling even harder. "And that *who* knows enough to have done *what*, *where*, and *when*, and they also have a *why*!"

"Violet's not the only one who told us produce sales were down because of the FEEL Contest."

The boys raced up to the farmers' market entrance and skidded their bikes to a stop, but the gate was locked, and all the stalls were empty. They spotted a handwritten sign:

CLOSED FOR BLOCK PARTY
BACK TOMORROW

"I guess even the farmers don't want to miss the big party," Frank said.

Joe wheeled his bike around and started back in the other direction. "I bet that's where we'll find our suspect."

When the boys reached their block, it was already starting to fill up with people. There was a small stage with a DJ playing music, snow cone and cotton candy booths, and even carnival games. A sign hanging over the street read FEEL GOOD GARDEN PARTY.

Frank pointed to a man and a woman in matching Bayport Science Center T-shirts standing in front of the first yard on the block, making notes on their clipboards. "Those must be the judges. They've already started inspecting the gardens."

When the boys got closer, they could see badges around the adults' necks that said FEEL JUDGE.

As more and more people showed up to join the party, the boys hopped off their bikes. They didn't want to run anyone over.

"I think I might know where we can find our culprit," Joe said.

Frank was already pushing his bike down the

street before Joe had even told him their destination. "It's hard for crooks to resist going back to the scene of the crime."

As the brothers approached their end of the block, they could see both Vic and Audrika still working away next door to each other, trying to tidy things up before the judges arrived. Both gardens were still pretty, with lots of green plants and colorful flowers, but they weren't nearly as spectacular as they had been before the sabotage. Audrika had tried to fill the empty spaces where all the huge cabbages had been, but you could tell something was missing. And Vic's tall trellises looked especially empty without all the cucumbers climbing up them.

Across the street, a tall, lanky man in a plaid shirt and a baseball cap was talking to one of the Hardys' neighbors. He kept glancing over his shoulder toward Vic's and Audrika's houses. When he did, the boys could see the smiling cartoon carrot stitched onto the cap and a pair of bushy eyebrows beneath the brim.

"Farmer Phil," Joe said under his breath.

The next time Phil turned to glance at Vic and Audrika, the Hardy brothers were standing right in front of him.

Farmer Phil took a surprised step backward. "Oh, um, hey, Joe. Hey, Frank. Great party, right?"

"Not for everyone," Frank said, looking across the street at Audrika and Vic.

Phil chuckled nervously. "Oh yeah. That woodchuck problem you were telling me about."

"Only, it turns out woodchucks weren't the real problem," Joe said.

"They, um, weren't?" Phil started fidgeting with his hat.

"We solved the woodchuck problem when I put up my Woodchuck Defense System and Joe put out the fruit buffet to keep the critters happy," Frank explained. "It turns out there was a different kind of pest."

"There was?" Phil started slowly backing away.

But Joe wasn't going to let the farmer get away. "Yeah, one with a reason to sabotage the FEEL Contest, because it was bad for their business."

"They heard about the woodchucks and decided they'd use them as cover to sabotage the neighborhood's best gardens and blame it on the critters," Frank said, picking up the story.

"They did?" Phil took another couple of steps back, but Joe and Frank kept following him until he bumped into a neighbor's fence. "Oof!"

"Do you know how our spoilsport knew there was a woodchuck problem?" Joe asked.

Phil shook his head.

"Because we told him," Frank said. "Sound familiar?"

This time, Phil shook his head so hard, his hat fell off.

Joe knelt to pick it up and dusted it off. "Turns out he's been our overripe fruit hookup from the start. We even told him bananas were the most popular item in the woodchuck buffet, so he knew exactly what to use as bait to lure them into our friends' gardens." Joe handed the hat to his brother.

"Those friends just happen to have the best gardens on the block," Frank said, offering the hat back to Farmer Phil. "Or they did, until you sabotaged them."

"Who—what—I—no—you—I'd—me—never!" Phil had gone pale.

"You told us you weren't worried about the contest costing you business because you had a hunch you'd have your customers back soon," Joe pressed. "Now we know why you were so confident."

When Frank glanced back across the street, the judges were in front of Vic's house. Vic stared up at them with puppy-dog eyes as they examined the empty trellis where his cucumbers had been. One of the judges sighed and shook his head before making a note on his clipboard. Vic's lip quivered as the pair left and continued next door to Audrika's garden.

Phil winced and clutched his hat to his chest.

"So much for your *Phil*osophy, huh? You talk about growing our community, eating local, and not wasting food. I guess that doesn't include local kids' cucumbers, peppers, and cabbages." Frank peered back across the street at Audrika, who was fidgeting in front of her missing cabbage patch, trying to keep the judges from noticing the gaps. It didn't work. The female judge walked around her, looked down at the cabbage-less soil, pursed her lips, and made a note on her clipboard.

"My Philos—" Phil stopped as Audrika and Vic both came out onto the sidewalk. Their heads were down, and it looked like Vic was holding back tears. Phil hung his own head. "It's supposed to be all about the importance of locally grown food, and there's nothing more local than a person's own yard." He stared at the smiling carrot on his cap. "The last time you picked up fruit from me, I said I didn't have any ripe bananas to spare. I lied. I saved them so I could lure the woodchucks into your neighbors' gardens."

"They're your neighbors too," Frank reminded him.

Phil gulped. "I got the idea when you first told me you had a woodchuck problem. I was so worried about my business, I sabotaged kids who were doing the exact thing I believe in most. My *Phil*osophy is about sustainable food and friendship. But I haven't been a very good friend."

Phil watched as Audrika went over to the fence the kids had put up together, sat next to Vic, and offered him a handful of blueberries from her garden. He sniffled, took one, and smiled.

"By ruining the best gardens and blaming the woodchucks, I thought I could discourage people from gardening, so more of them would have to buy their veggies from me again," Phil continued. "Vic's parents used to be my best customers before the family started gardening. I hadn't thought about who I was hurting—or how I was hurting the things I believe in."

"The cucumber culprit comes clean," Joe said.

"Too bad the damage is already done." Frank glared at Phil. "Audrika and Vic will probably both lose the contest because of it."

"I know it doesn't make up for what I've done, but I can give them all the seedlings they want from my own farm to replace the plants that were destroyed," Phil offered.

"You're right," Frank said. "It doesn't make up for the damage." He paused as Phil ducked his head even lower. "But it is a start. And there might be something else you can do."

Joe saw Frank watching the judges and snapped his fingers. "Follow us!" he said to Phil. "You can tell the judges exactly why our friends' gardens aren't as glorious as they should be."

After the judges were done inspecting all the gardens— including the Hardys'—all the neighbors gathered around the stage for the big announcements. Frank, Joe, Audrika, Vic, and Violet stood together as the judges read off the winners and honorable mentions for each category. Finally, only the top prize was left, and none of their names had been called.

"Sorry, bro," Joe said, putting his arm around Frank's shoulder. "I know how much you wanted an honorable mention."

The judge cleared her throat. "And the winner of the grand prize for Top Edible Lawn goes to . . . Drumroll please, DJ!"

"I don't think either of us are going to win, Vic," Audrika said quietly.

"It's okay," Vic replied. "We both know how amazing our gardens really are, even if the judges didn't get to see all our hard work."

The drumroll rattled through the DJ's speakers, followed by the judge's voice:

"Vic Blake!"

Vic looked up in surprise. "I won?"

"And . . . ," the other judge said, taking the microphone. "Audrika Khaleel!"

Audrika did a double take. "We won?"

The judges beamed down at them from the stage.

"Due to special circumstances, we're proud to have two worthy winners!" the second judge added.

"We won!" Vic and Audrika shouted together.

"WOO-HOO!" Frank, Joe, and Violet cheered, and started jumping up and down along with their friends.

"Free pickles for the champs!" Violet announced.

"I may not have gotten the honorable mention I was hoping for, but this is even better," Frank said. He glanced at the back of the crowd, where Farmer Phil stood by himself.

Phil smiled shyly and tipped his cap.

There was a buzzing sound from the stage as the first judge took the microphone again.

"A certain mysterious matter has been brought to our attention, so we have decided to award a special prize in a brand-new gardening category to"—the judge paused—"Frank and Joe Hardy!"

"Huh?" the brothers said at the same time.

"Please give a round of applause for our winners of the Garden Gumshoe Award!"

Audrika, Vic, and Violet burst into cheers.

"You guys sure are the best veggie investigators in town." Vic threw his arms around the brothers' shoulders, while Violet handed them each a celebratory pickle.

Audrika smiled. "I never realized how much gardening and detecting are alike. Sometimes it's a real puzzle figuring out what a plant needs for it to grow strong. Just like solving a case!"

"And all of us know how to dig around to unearth the answers." Frank took a triumphant bite of his pickle.

Joe grinned at their neighbors. "With your green thumbs and our mystery minds, we can solve any plant predicament!"

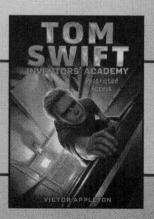

READ & LEARN

with *simon* kids

Keep your child reading, learning, and having fun with Simon Kids!

A one-stop shop where you can
find downloadable resources, watch interactive author videos, browse books by reading level, and more!

Visit us at
SimonandSchusterPublishing.com/ReadandLearn/

And follow us @SimonKids

Looking for another great book?
Find it
IN THE MIDDLE.

Fun, fantastic books for kids
in the in-be**TWEEN** age.

IntheMiddleBooks.com

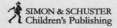